MICK: A CELESTIAL DRAMA

ALSO BY JIM KELLEHER

Quarry (poems, 2008)

MICK: A CELESTIAL DRAMA

Jim Kelleher 8/13/2011

For Vita Muia —
Treasure is in the heart.

Antrim House
Simsbury, Connecticut

Copyright © 2011 by Jim Kelleher

Except for short selections reprinted for purposes of
book review, all reproduction rights are reserved.
Requests for permission to replicate should
be addressed to the publisher.

Library of Congress Control Number: 2011909820

ISBN: 978-1-936482-05-4

Printed & bound by United Graphics, Inc.

First Edition, 2011

Cover photograph: Jake Anderson

Photograph of author: Jack "Red Sock" Sheedy

Book Design: Rennie McQuilkin

Antrim House
860.217.0023
AntrimHouse@comcast.net
www.AntrimHouseBooks.com
21 Goodrich Road, Simsbury, CT 06070

Mick is dedicated to my teachers: Alicia, Anne Marie,
Anne, Carol, Charles, Dave, Frank, Gerry,
Gray, Harold, Jane, Jeff, Joan, Judith,
Langston, Maxine, Michael,
Robert, Stephen, Susan
and William B.

Thank you!

ACKNOWLEDGEMENT

Poems presented herein first appeared in
The Country and Abroad, Litchfield County Times,
and *From Under the Bridges of America* (anthology).

TABLE OF CONTENTS

A Note from the Author / viii

"Alfonso's Poem" / ix

Cast of Characters / 3

Stage Sets / 4

Prologue / 5

Act I: Take Me Out to the Ballgame / 7

Act 2: Peanuts & Crackerjacks / 29

Act 3: I Don't Care If I Never Come Back / 43

Act 4: Seventh Inning Stretch / 59

Act 5: Last Licks / 71

Act 6: Extra Innings / 83

About the Author / 93

Colophon / 94

A Note from the Author

Treasure exists in the heart as much as in the wallet or a Dunkin' Donuts cup. When I saw Jake Anderson's photo of Alfonso Dagonzo in his book *Homeless Souls*, I knew Alfonso was right for my own book's cover. And when I read Alfonso's poem, I knew it explained Mick, my protagonist.

Truth is stranger, and harder, than fiction. Do we dream to escape reality, or to make a better reality? Are dreams our destination? How do we get there? And how do we help our friends for whom "things have gone wrong," as Alfonso says of his own life?

This book is my celestial dream. Like Alfonso's, "my hopes are strong." One of those hopes is that proceeds from this book, which will be donated to homeless men, women, and families, will help them survive on the streets.

Treasure, be it of gold or spirit, is what we give each other. It keeps us warm.

A thank-you to Jake for his photos and poems, and to Rennie for publishing *Mick*. Finally, thank you to you, for reading along.

Alfonso's Poem

My talent is not to be
gathering dust
My hopes are strong
My career move is
    still bright
My projects can't take
    me so long
I am looking on the
    bright side
I feel a lot of inner pain
Things have gone wrong

by Alfonso Daganzo

Cast of Characters

Mick Monahan: dishevelled and raggy, needs a shave, red streaks in white hair

Officer Ortiz: a huge brown man in a blue police uniform

Richie: Mick's son, appearing only as a head, the rest of his body remaining in black

Saint Peter: old man with long beard and traditional staff

Maureen: Mick's daughter, aka "Little Mo," a girl 13 with bosoms and iPod

Lucille: Mick's wife, an aged beauty with décolletage, face smeared with ash

Billy Gorilla: Mick's doppelganger — never speaks but dances around Mick in his gorilla suit

Sarge: NYPD officer with stripes

Mr. Greenbeans: tall and angry grocer in white smock

Homeboys: five white toughs, menacing, with cut-off T-shirts and muscles

Nuns: old women in black habits with gold crosses

ER doctor, nurse: he in white gown, she in blue scrubs

STAGE SETS

The stage is divided into stage left, stage center, and stage right. Only one section is lit at any time. An angel in white appears to announce the title of each poem before it is recited.

Stage left is always 109th St. and Amsterdam Ave. A sign says "109th St." There is a cardboard Maytag box with "Home of Champions" painted on it. Also Mick's pack, his pint bottle and his shoebox.

Stage right is always Heaven. Red neon letters, strung across, read "Heaven." St. Peter's staff is always present, and a representation of a red Hummer.

Stage center is the variable stage: it changes to represent Central Park, a subway car, "the Bleachers," an ER, a convent, etc. The place is identified by a cardboard sign and one or two changeable props; e.g., the convent might be represented by a big gold cross, the subway car by a line of seats, the ER by a steel gurney, Central Park by huge plants, the "Bleachers" by a hard bench, baseball mitt, etc. After each poem, the lights dim to announce a new poem. After a complete act, all is darkness for a time. There is one intermission, after Act 3.

Prologue

Dear Audience

(Mick is alone before drawn curtain. As is the case at the start of each poem, an angel in white announces the title.)

I never planned to scribble a play
in verse. No shit — I barely survived

high school English. There's nothing
schooly about me.

Then screams
from horny wife and two brats

drove me past the Edge, smack
into Smirnoff. Homeless, one-handed,

(Enter Ortiz)
I was found out by beat cop Ortiz —
he kept watch on my cardboard.

(Enter Richie)
My boy Richie appeared in dreams.
His red head ruined my sleep. DTs.

(Enter St. Peter and Billy Gorilla)
Saint Peter? And Billy Gorilla?
I can't explain this narrative,

(Enter Lucille and Maureen)
not Lucille's laments, our troubled
colleen Maureen, pregnant,

not the hidden baseball cards
and flashbacks I had along the way.

I had sabotaged and quit my family,
my blues chalked on subway cars.

Holocaust may descend on all of us —
ice caps melting, AIDS, Arabia flaming.

It's enough to make me slug a triple scotch.
But put your drug of choice aside

and please, review my story —
the keening of a dad's heart,

my son's disaster, our search, and 9-11.
The action goes down in New York City

and Heaven, two impossible places.
Thanks be to God and Yogi Berra.

(All exit.)

ACT 1

TAKE ME OUT TO THE BALLGAME

Mick Monahan's Odyssey

(Set: 109th Street. Mick crawls from his Maytag box, points and gesticulates toward Officer Ortiz, who towers over him in his blue uniform, shining his flashlight at Mick and at the inscription "Home of Champions" painted on the box in sloppy black capital letters. A raggy backpack and pint bottle lie outside the box.)

His black shoes kick my blue hand and I cough
blood and phlegm. My froze-up fingers curl
outside the cardboard. I was sleeping one off
in a Maytag washer crate, bothering no one,
snoring oldies but goodies like an iPod.
Then Blue Man comes and busts my dream,
my snowy, tinsel, Christmas dream —

Gram roasts a turkey, a clove ham with pineapples.
She serves big steamy bowls of green beans.
My older sister Maureen shrieks. She feeds me
Hershey Candy Kisses. Mom has framed
my first grade Holy Cross photos and Santa surprises me
with a rare Mickey Mantle bubblegum card.
I collect Yankees and Dodgers in shoeboxes.

(Mick opens the shoebox at his feet, looks at several baseball cards. Then he secretively returns the shoebox to his pack.)

Then Cop tells me to show my driver's license
and I tell him to fuck off. I sold my Dodge Dart
before they made it Daimler-Benz. Who the fuck
is Daimler? Who is Benz? I am Slammin' Mick
Monahan, grew up right here on 109th Street,
Amsterdam Avenue, Manhattan. Spanish Harlem
to you, stupid. Why don't you leave me alone?

I am block stickball champ! I can hit three
manhole covers! I broomstick Spaldeens so hard I split
'em in half! I shatter fourth-story
windows — I am King of Ground-rule Doubles!
I rammed a pink rubber rocket that ricocheted
off a yellow Checker and stuck right in the grate
of this black subway vent! Jesus, I got no wallet.

(Mick rummages in his pockets for his wallet, then begins to nod off. Officer Ortiz nudges Mick's hand with his black shoe.)

Cop keeps kicking my bluefish hand, waking me.
I advise him sleeping in public sucks, but it's safe.
Kings and Sinners won't bust me up or torch me.
Do I want a shelter? I was robbed in one. Homer
had his ship, I say. This cardboard box is good for me.
(Sarge enters.)
Then his Sergeant yells, "Arrest him!" But he don't.
"He belongs in a shelter," says NYPD 1831 Ortiz.

The blue and white paddy wagon pulls right on my curb.
Sarge arrests me. He's no jolly Saint Nick, but
the jail bus is warm. I wave *adios* to to Officer Ortiz.
I close my eyes and I remember Moose Skowron,
Elston Howard, Hank Bauer's rifle arm. I see Micky
and Yogi hitting home runs off the foul pole.
I taste sweet potatoes and cranberries, and I am home.

The Tombs

(A sign reads "The Tombs." In his cell, Mick speaks to himself wistfully, looks up as he mentions his kids.)

I smell like shit and vomit when I wake.
I'm a booze lump — itchy junkies don't touch me.

Crackheads and smackers, pimps and fag queens
don't touch me. I sleep on my coat, my pack is my pillow.

Richie, I dream of you and your coke-sucking mom
and little Mo, my baby Maureen. Oh sweetie...

The A Train

(A subway car. A sign reads "A Train." Mick rocks back and forth as he delivers his lines, looking upward as he says "dad" and "son," then looking away.)

Out of jail six a.m. Free to roam the cobbles,
bum a token, buy a pint, ride the A Train home.

I am rockin' and sleepin' and smellin' it up.
I am warm as a cockroach under the tub.

No one looks at me. They read *The Daily News*,
study the signs, make believe they don't see.

Are they scared I'll rob 'em? No, just afraid
they'll get old like me. At least I know who I was.

I was a Torrington Twister, and a dad too.
I was a 'Nam vet, a hero to you, son.

I got 109th Street to get to, my Maytag crate.
My ship sailed — and left you, Richie. I left you.

Richie Greets Saint Peter

(Heaven. Saint Peter does not speak, just waves his staff. Richie's red-haired head, which is all of him that can be seen, does the talking.)

Wham! I hit the truck, my head
breaks off and...here I am. This is —
Heaven? It's shiny here.
I'm from the Lower East Side.
You ever been there? I think I seen you.
Hey, does my sister Maureen miss me?
Where's my cell phone? Is my mom here?
My dad sure ain't. He's drunk somewhere.

How long did it take you to grow that beard?
Can I — it feels like Brillo.
Hey, why am I here? I'm fifteen, for Christ's
sake! Oh...sorry. Okay, okay, I stole
the Lexus, on Fifth I guess —
So I was speeding, so what!
So I submarined the Kenworth. Shit!
My head bounced off like a softball.

(His hand reaches up from his blacked-out body below, to be sure the head is there)

Where I live, I hate it. Even the trees
are dirty. You ever been on Avenue D?
You sure? I search the Bowery for Dad,
sometimes. You look like a homeless
with that beard. You ever shave? Okay,
okay! I was dealing coke. Savin' money
to buy a home someplace, Westchester,
someplace clean, get us out of the project.
Don't tell me I fucked up — I know it.

Listen, old man, think whatever you want.
Don't wave your stick at me! I stole stuff
'cause we needed it. After dad split
Ma got a dishwasher job in the Towers.
She got into crack, she got blown up...
She here? Ain't seen none of my friends yet.
You let junkies in? It's expensive, huh?
I got credit cards — you got Nintendo?

Lilttle Sister

(The Convent. Mr. Green Beans looms stage right, yells his lines. Richie is spotlit stage left, also yelling his lines. A gold crucifix is prominent overhead. Maureen speaks, holding her iPod.

I remember when my brother and me
almost got arrested. We gobbled
cherries in Stop and Shop — Richie
stuck a Bumblebee tuna down his pants.

(Richie, stage left, speaks his own lines, which Maureen, Little Sister, merely mouths.)

Then Richie peeled an organic banana.
"I think they taste better," he told me.
I saw Green Beans. I called him that
'cause he sprayed the lettuce and beets.

(Green Beans, stage right, also speaks his own lines, which Maureen once again merely mouths.)

"THIEVES! YOU LITTLE CUNT!"
Mean Beans roared like King Kong.
He gave me hairy eyeballs — ten feet tall!
"YOU'RE ARRESTED!"

"FUCK YOU, YOU SHITHEAD!"
Richie yelled and pulled a salami from his jacket.
He whacked Mean Beans on his hand.
His fat thumb crooked like a dead pigeon.

Richie snatched me up and we ran.
We escaped to the East River and circled
back to Avenue D. We sneaked down
the rusty steel stairs to our boiler room.

"Don't worry, Mo. He's a shitty green giant."
Richie wrapped me in his Harley jacket.
He made us tuna and salami sandwiches.
Then we both fell asleep on our mattress.

Home Run

(The Bleachers, marked by a sign overhead and a wood bench. Props: a bat, a ball, a Pepsi sign. Mick speaks.)

When I was sixteen
I could slam a fastball

over the Pepsi sign.
Today I can't lift

a Louisville Slugger.
I want to forget.

I want to forget
all of it.

What I see
when I drink

is a baseball spinning —
the red seams on the ball.

I see myself
smashing it deep.

I see my team,
Billy Martin swearin'.

Get me a whiskey
and beer chaser,

get me a boilermaker.
Just get me a drink.

I can't hit
shit.

Billy G.

(109th Street. Billy Gorilla appears in gorilla suit, prances around Mick, who speaks.)

I know a gorilla.
He humps me in my sleep.

Billy (his name is Billy)
humps me with this curse —

"Stand up, you stinky drunk."
He slobbers worse and worse.

He's huge, like debt,
rank like shit,

fast and monstrous noisy
like the A Train.

His breath is onions.
He's big.

He never hurries —
he takes his sweet gorilla time.

"I'm yours forever," he says.
He smiles his wet gorilla smile.

I try to push him away,
I pound his hairy face.

In the mirror *(Mick stares into a hand mirror)*
he stares at me.

"I'm Boss," he says.
"Throw up."

I wish to Christ I could kill him —
he finished off my bourbon.

Lucille in Heaven

(Heaven. Lucille puts a hand to her ear to hear Mick crying out from the dark.)

Swabbing pots on the eighty-ninth floor
when the first plane hit and I felt the heat

(whoosh, so quick!), I heard Mick —
"I'm drunk, I did it, I'm sorry, I admit it."

That's what he said, the prick.
He walked out, left us broke, sick,

Rich on my hip, Mo tearing my nipple,
me with no welfare but two yowly brats

and an AWOL mate, a stinking drunk,
and rats in the kitchen and under the bed,

and him sucking pints and my old parents
dead. Oh, I don't mind telling you (you can

give a flying fuck or not, I sure don't)
I did what I could and what I could not,

so what? I started inhaling an innocent
line, then sold my ass for milk and rent

and the marriage died. My great tits sagged.
When we met, Mick called me Luscious

Lucille. But I swear he lived in Doyle's Pub,
not our flat. I lost him to Chivas and the Johnny

Walkers, red and black. How could I compete
with his hot cognac and Jim Beam?

I miss my kids but to hell with Mick — Saint
Peter assigned me this twelve-step suite.

Folderol, Folderol

(Heaven. Lucille's soliloquy is spoken as she wanders.)

White roses with black thorns,
what use breasts for my babies?
Mick stumbled away and we scoured
crumbs, hoarded graham crackers.
I'd have crowned him if I could
but had no muscle to crush a roach.

Since 9/11 Peter has been my confessor.
He blessed my ash from the burning
Towers. Muslim imams preach a martyr's
play — but those rabid Arabs
flew like bats with rabies.
Feed them arsenic, I say.

Peter says I should forgive, I must —
but my heart hits the firewall. Desires
died black in Ground Zero's ashtray.
I want a Celtic grace, a soft way to confess —
I would do my murdered life over: Mick,
my babies gone astray. Hopes,

those broken dreams I poach, scramble
in Heaven as maybes: maybe
a failed mother, maybe a crackhead
whose habit pushed Mick away. Give me
bloodhounds and detectives. I should
have thrived. I want answers.

Is there forgiveness for all?
Lovers' dry hearts split like wood.
I met a priest covered in burning blood —
he said life or death brings you to your knees.
Finally you have nothing to say.
Your corpse, if lucky, will fit a box.

Ortiz at Ground Zero

(109th Street. Ortiz stands before Mick's cardboard. Mick, inside, is not visible. Ortiz stares off-stage as he remembers 9/11.)

Crawling through voids, coughing
the gray chalk dust of lead, glass,
asbestos, concrete, petrochemicals.
Chasing off punk souvenir-seekers.
Even big city rats won't work there.

The infrared never spikes, just
registers — metal, rubber, smolder.
It melts the rubber off boot heels.
I stuff ears, noses, hands, feet
into plastic body bags and baggies.

Eighty hours since The Towers crumbled.
I'm bleary. Searching eight to dawn
after my scheduled six-to-six tour.
My partner O'Brien is still missing.
Is anyone alive?

Mick's Pigeons

*(Mick sits on a park bench and throws imaginary crumbs
to birds at his feet. Overhead, a sign reads "Central Park.")*

I didn't want to leave the kids. It just happened.
My head is splitting, my coat full of dinner,

hard Kaiser rolls. Dropping sweet crumbs
off this Central Park bench, feeding my birds,

my buds, my pigeons! O lyrical shit-makers,
cooers, dirty city doves! Who needs parakeets?

Democratic pigeons, patriots, gray, white, blue
and black, my multi-racial posse, my crew.

Eat, my lovelies, grow big and powerful like me.
You will be heroes and sluggers too. Little Yankees.

We Are Family

(Heaven. Richie pauses before delivering the last line.)

There ain't no crime to do in Heaven.
What I really want is to visit mom
and Mo, kid sister. Nowhere. So
I been watchin' re-runs of "Charley's Angels"
'cause I like those smart babes
when Peter's not lookin'.

Ma used to buy me Breyer's
Neapolitan. Even when
she had sweats. No pork chops but
always Neapolitan.

I remember Labor Day.
Mick took us all to a Bo Sox game.
He bought bench seats
in the right field bleachers.
Yankee stadium rocked. Mick was yellin'
"You suck, ump!" Ma slapped him shut.
Mind the kids, she said. So Mick
got me popcorn and a Wilson mitt.

They was kissin' then, I remember.
Baby Mo was in her hot wheels stroller and
Mick's foot somehow loosened the wheels
so it rolled faster and faster and Ma broke
a high heel on the pavement chasin' it.
She sailed it right past Dad's head.

Then Dad went drunk and Ma started cookin'.
I figured I was boss — started dealin' ounces.
Maui Zowie mary jane bought our pizza.

Meanwhile I was Mo's bodyguard in P.S. 20 —
but horny homeboys jumped her.

Homeboys

(The Convent. Maureen (Mo) rises from her cot to look out an imaginary window, recalling the rape. To one side, five menacing homeboys flex their muscles.)

Danny got his bucktooth grin
and Bobby got red pimples.
They boss us homeroom girls
'cause they got big muscles.

Danny leads his whole crew in,
Billy locks the bathroom,
Ronnie kills the lights,
Sammy pushes me into the stall.

Then Danny spits his bucktooth grin
and Bobby sticks his runny pimples
right in my face. Wrestler arms,
pit bull breath. He forces me open.

Then Danny's crew take turns,
do the sex wheel on me, show me
who's boss.

Richie's Verdict

(Richie in Heaven)

Protection! I don't need protection!
I got all the muscle I need on Avenue D —
the homeboys...
(Richie listens to St. P's pantomimed words.)

What? You said *probation*?
What's up with that?
OW!
*(St. P whacks Richie with his staff.
R's head jerks back.)*

(Richie listens to more pantomimed words.)
Fuck! Thirty days!
I don't see mom for thirty days?
(Richie listens again.) What about Mick?
You want me to talk to him in *dreams*?
Are you nuts?
OW!

What about my sister Mo? *(Listens again.)*
Mo's in a convent? She's *thirteen*!
Her *angel* made this deal? Show me —
I ain't seen no angels.

OW!

*%#$&##!!! *(Richie swears and jumps around.)*

OW! OW!
(Richie exits with St. P in hot pursuit.)

Little Sister Wishes

(The Convent. Nuns enter and hold crosses high over Mo's head. She clutches her iPod.)

I wish my brother was here.
Or even my baby's father but
whoever he was, he hurt me.
I don't remember Mick but

I was named for his sister,
Aunt Maureen. If only Richie
got here — he would bring
Harry Potter books, he would —

I wish on this black Bible
I was home on Avenue D.
My belly's swelled and I'm scared.
What a convent of trouble I'm in.

Sisters hang gold crosses
and black blessings over me.
I wish I escape, I wish
I play my Foo Fighters CD.

Last night I dreamed ten crows
cawing in the white birch tree.
They cawed and cawed at me.
I caught and burned them.

Snotty Stuck-Ups

(109th Street. Mick howls at the imaginary moon.)

You think 'cause I stink in a crate
I don't rate, I don't think or understand?
To hell with you, George Bush. Bite me.
I got six "Extra Effort" blue ribbons
from Blessed Jesus Sacred Heart High School
'cause I passed English.

I could write essays like Montana.
Rhymes flew off my pen like sparrows
in Central Park before muggings.
I did graduate — I was a Lariat.
I did villanovas, Sicilian sonnuts,
sextinas, phantoms, limicks.

I wrote a letter to Norman Rockwell.
I mailed a Christmas card to Laura Bush.
I told her forget flipping cowboys
and see us homeless get pea soup.
'Cause we served. 'Cause real patriots
get black and blue. And I ain't complaining.

Colors

(109th Street. Mick scribbles on a pad.)

Yo Norm,

    I never thought I'd say it but —
I need you back, you shit.

    Browns and blacks and mean greens
grab me — camouflage colors — brown shit,
black blood, green bile.

    I remember *The Runaway*, your cover
on the *Sat. Evening Post*. I was your freckled
white boy with the red bag of treasures, GI Joes,
F-15 jets. Big blue cop counseled me at the soda
fountain. Smiley clerk, elbows propped, listened
to our chat. That old pedophile.

    Your boy grew old, lost his pluck.
Got a close-up feel for Agent Orange, right hand
amputated for Uncle Sam. So what? George
went off, bombed Iraq, slashed rich folks' taxes,
dissed Ayatollah and that North Korean whack —
what's up with his smack? Oil? Oil, oil, oil!

    Buy your American flag right here, folks!
I'm a workin' vet, I'm a flag-wavin' Stars & Stripes
seller! For one green dollar show off America!

    Yo, Norm! Paint me. If you got the reds & whites,
I got the blues.

Mick.

CURTAIN

ACT 2

PEANUTS & CRACKERJACKS

Net Worth

(109th Street. Mick sits outside his cardboard on the pavement. He pulls items from his pack, holds them, studies them, then speaks while staring into his hand mirror.)

My turquoise sparklers that mowed the ladies —
bloodshot eyeballs now, dull black marbles.

Carrot hair thinning, wavy white,
busted spider veins on my nose. I hate what I am.

My right hand's a hook, left digits froze up,
stumpy peanuts like Yogi's catcher fingers

except no World Series rings, no fame, no fans,
no glory, just a tough-shit story and a pint of Cuervo

stashed in my pack with my shoebox, Yankee shirt,
wool blanket and socks and Richie & Mo's baby shoes.

Night Sweats

(109th Street. Richie appears stage left without speaking, his head spotlighted. Mick stares at him as he rants.)

I'm hallucinatin'! Or I got DTs — It's
the tequila — donkey piss poison.

That you, Richie? I swear you got the right
red hair! I hate these fucking nightmares.

I dreamed last night you died. I swore,
I busted up the subway, pissed Central Park.

(Mick listens) You like it up there? It's clean —
up there? I don't believe this shit. What about Mo?

(Mick listens again.) Pregnant? She's a baby herself!
Don't play with my brain. You're nothing, a ghost!

(Mick listens again)
I should fight back? What sort of son would say that!
My boy would agree — I did not quit!

You don't know shit. *(Richie grabs Mick by the shirt collar.)*
Let me go! *(Richie fades off stage. Mick pulls himself together.)*

Look at me — soaked like a bar sponge.
I'll never trust José Cuervo again.

From now on, only scotch and rye.
Only good American beer and wine.

Richie was too real — he scared me shitless.
It's withdrawal, I think. Got to get me a drink.

The Dance

*(109th Street. Billy in gorilla suit may
repeat Mick's words if a director wishes.)*

Holy Litany — Lucille,
why did you leave me?

At least booze loves me
and Billy, my gorilla.

"Tough shit," he says.
He eats bananas,

he hugs me.
"Puke your guts," he says.

Kids with AIDS,
Bush, Cheney, Bin Laden.

Can't get food stamps,
welfare, meds.

How cold and old I feel
no one knows.

Billy knows:
"Puke your guts," he says.

He drools,
pats me.

"I'll be loving you," he sings,
"each night I get the chance."

He revels in our sodomy,
he whirls me in our dance.

Bad Dreams

(109th Street. As Mick speaks, Richie's head in a far corner of the stage nods and pantomimes speech.)

How did you find me again?
Global positioning?

(Mick listens to Richie's pantomimed question.)
I left you and Lucille, Richie,
because I was a sot.

I thought I would die and you
with me. I was afraid.

You got your truth. Now get out.
Do I ask you to show up?

(Mick listens again.)
You never gave up on *me*? *(Listens)*
I'm a bum! What sort of answer is that?

(Mick listens again.)
All right, all right, I won't swear.
Jesus, you're a stubborn kid.

What else? Make it quick. *(Listens)*
You want to know about my *life?*

A story? *(Listens)* You like "Goldfinger"?
"The Cow Pissed the Moon"?

Grand Auto

(109th Street. Mick speaks, Richie's head moving in response.)

When I was sixteen I stole a Caddy — rammed it
on a pole by the El, 125th Street near the Hudson.

I split before the gas tank exploded,
went running to play ball on 110th and Riverside

when the Kings swept down the hill, charging me.
It didn't matter what color us gangs were.

Race was a cover-up, like a flag. What counted
was you smashed a kid, hurt him bad.

Niggers chased me across the West Side Highway.
I almost jumped into the Hudson but knew enough

not to drown, so I sprinted to 96th, lungs crying.
I had pistons, Rich — I could run. I figured

they'd throw me in if they caught me,
so shit-scared I outran everyone.

Next day *Los Locos* took me hostage in the gym.
Miguel cracked eggs on my skull. He tied me

like a Vietcong. He wanted turf.
El jefe, loco, un hombre peligroso.

My own gang had to ransom me —
a case of Bud caused his shit-eating grin.

At least he had no gun. Not like *your* homeboys.
But look, I'm nuts you stole that Lexus, lost

your head. It's my fault. *(Mick shakes his head in remorse.)*
I wish I'd crashed that Caddy into iron instead!

Groovin'

(109th Street. Continuation of previous scene.)

You understand me? I guess you got
life's hard lugs from me. Crapped out like me.

I was born cocked and you guessed right —
booze sucks up families. My dad was a roaring

drunk, and his dad, your great grandfather, rode
around Tralee on a white horse bullshitting

colleens, bless him. When I hit eighteen
I worked construction. Weekends

I ushered at the Fillmore East, a psychedelic
palace on 2nd Avenue. LSD launched weekend

flights — double sets by Jefferson Airplane,
the Youngbloods, Jerry Garcia and the Dead.

In '68 the Fillmore floated in hash
and pot. Blue clouds hung in strobes.

I ushered heads to seats, flashed my light
while they lit their bowls. They tipped me

fat joints. The acid coursed and eased, swelled
like slide guitars and bongos. *The Who,*

Hendrix, Chuck Berry, B.B. King, Fats Domino.
You know Santana's sound? He's still around.

Yasgur's Farm: The Grateful Dead

(109th Street. Continuation of previous scene.)

Richie, I split New York in a VW bus,
      dumped it four miles from Yasgur's.
Us Fillmore crew set the stage, rigged
      the sound and strobes.

I climbed the scaffold stage right,
      thirty feet over monster speakers.
The crowd freaked me — hundreds of thousands
      crammed in the bowl.

I dropped mescaline. I was rushing. I had to sprawl.
      A French photographer
bribed me with a ball of hash. I let her up,
      all the way, on my private scaffold.

The kids booed the warnings: did acid,
      orange meth crystals.
Bum trips went to the med tent.
      The crowd was bumming — like me. I was

full of vomit. I just held onto the pipes,
      watched the Big Dipper,
thousands of tiny joints being lit in Yasgur's meadow,
      red sparks passing hand to hand.

Wake me up in the morning dew, my honey, wake me
      up in the morning dew, today...
I watched Garcia pick notes, felt the crowd
      settle back. The amphitheater

exhaled. Pot blew past me, so heavy, sweet —
    I felt my scaffold sway in the breeze.
I was afraid they'd rush the stage, Richie —
    they loved the Dead.

I kept my green Woodstock windbreaker
    with its logo: the dove
on the guitar. Joe Cocker offered me a hundred for it.
    What am I, stupid?

Higher Education

(109th Street. Continuation of previous scene.)

I got my first job out of Sacred Heart,
unloading semis — sheetrock, steel studs.

I overslept and Andy Wisneski said
my union apprentice job was dead.

Our steward from County Down jumped
to defend me — the Monahan name,

my wavy red hair — he kept me in it,
the Brotherhood of Carpenters and Joiners.

Pat said punch in on time. Keep your yak
shut, and work, work...

I put up the Gulf Tower on Columbus Circle,
put up ceilings whole city blocks long.

Nights were full of freighters running the Hudson,
Manhattan lit up for Christmas — golds,

silvers, reds, greens. December 24th was
swearing, sweating, fitting tiles...

I lugged Buds for the boys at lunch,
slugged whiskeys in Dingo's later...

I built my shoulders humping sheetrock.
Andy called me Whiskers, Abe Lincoln...

He gave me third year wages but
I signed with the Twisters. He shrugged,

wrote me a lay-off slip so I could collect —
"Kid, we're rats here. You're a baby rat."

Twisting the Night Away

(109th Street. Continuation of previous scene.)

When I signed with Torrington I was big.
I could slug, had sheetrock shoulders.

Magic Mike Puzzo managed us,
made runs from squat — a walk, bunt,

stolen base. Stick your ass out,
get hit by a pitch. Suicide squeezes.

Puzzo's strategy was small ball.
I wanted to hit home runs.

He benched me for speed,
short guys who zipped the bases.

Like Billy Martin. Or that thief who
stole home, Maury Wills. I signed balls

down in the bullpen, bet big,
playin' five-card on the bus.

And us Torrington Twisters got twisted,
win or lose.

I signed for one year
but Magic Mike cut me short.

"Stick to bangin' nails," he said.
"Bangin' nails you got a future."

Then LBJ drafted me —
no signing bonus, no crackerjacks,

just boots and bodies on the ground
rotting like pork in rice paddies.

Lai Khe

(Continuation. Mick wears army helmet, holds an old rifle, walks back and forth before his cardboard, hallucinating.)

"Cherry Boy," they called me,
new to the steamy, leechy jungle.

Should have fragged the commander —
he sent us right into a kill zone.

The VC opened up, hiding in the shade.
In blinding sunshine

they exploded my hand. *(Mick holds up his claw.)*
Our jets roared low, too late,

too late the air vibrated — screams
and guts spilling everywhere,

napalm exploding at 2000 degrees,
fire, fire exploding hundred foot trees...

"Can anyone hear me?
Here, here — for Christ's sake."

Helo bubbles dropped body bags —
"Get his ass out of here."

They slaughtered sixty-one of us —
an ambush with AK-47s from the trees.

Us, the Black Lions, the Big Red,
shot up in the Iron Triangle

northwest of Saigon. I never saw
the VC sniped me. Fucking sneak! *(He spits.)*

CURTAIN

ACT 3

I Don't Care If I Never Come Back

Escape

(109th Street. Mick holds up an American flag. Billy mocks him.)

My plan —
sell flags,

write a song,
"The High Life."

Successes —
the Gulf Tower,

the Fillmore,
the Twisters.

I survived 'Nam,
I love my kids.

A sunny dream,
a human dolphin —

when Billy
slaps my head.

"Here,"
he says.

He rips my flag, *(Billy rips flag)*
he pees my bed,

leaves the floor
slick with shit.

No Way, Richie

(Heaven. Richie makes demands, is whacked with staff.)

I want to see Ma, right away.
A deal's a deal. Hey,
maybe we can negotiate —
and Mick wants to see Mo. *(St. P raises his arm.)*
I did *not* tell him she's in a convent!
I never get credit for trying!

OW! Okay, let's please discuss
my thirty day's probation.
I've been good —
no swearing, no blaspheming, no nookie.
There's no chances up here anyway.

OW! Okay! I won't say "nookie."
No nookie now. HEY, Don't swing your stick.

I've been talking to Mick in his dreams,
like you said, and listening with respect,
like you said.

If you let me see Lucille
she might tell me the truth.
I've been trying to straighten out *myself,*
but I feel like dirt about Mo —

I tried to be a dad for her
but I didn't see them homeboys coming.
I always screw up.

What do you mean "There's no way back"?
I should just chill? *(St. Peter nods approval.)*

Eduardo Ortiz, NYPD

(109th Street. Ortiz examines Mick's wallet, pulls out baseball cards.)

The drunk Sarge busted —
his wallet was wedged in his crate.
Now I know who Mick is.
Hey, there's no cash here,
just old baseball cards.
And — he's a vet! What a disgrace
to hole him up in the slammer.

Fact: I'll keep one eye out —
he's bound to come back,
they always do. Unless
his liver fails or a train
smacks him. These homeless drunks,
it's a bitch how they go.

Myself, I'm fucked —
I wouldn't arrest him. The brass
will have my head.
But I don't wear this badge
to lock up homeless.

I been down to Ground Zero
digging out the bones. My fingers are
blood sausage. I've worked the East Bronx,
the Market and the Zoo.
Now I'm supposed to be a blue cage
for our rats. Rat Keeper.
I refuse.

Pantoum of the Subway

(Subway car. Mick staggers as he speaks.)

My stop's 109th Street,
a local swing 'n sway.
I used to hop the turnstile
but I found a better way.

Strap-hangers swing 'n sway
legal. I drop slugs in token slots
'cause I found a better way.
Cop can't be everywhere.

I drop slugs in token slots
and lurch from car to car.
Cop can't be everywhere.
He don't know who you are.

I weave from car to car,
I sprawl seat to seat.
Who knows who you are —
all my rides are free.

I sprawl seat to seat.
I used to hop the turnstile —
got to ride for free!
Gettin' off — 109th Street.

Mission Plan

(Heaven. St. P's voice is loud and magisterial.)

Take Shakespeare there, our rough London bard.
Like Mick, he loved the ale and ladies. He prospered
by writing late, pleading forgiveness, praying hard.
It's never late to save a soul, even a heart despaired.

Surrender! Find friends, good works, a community.
Do the next right thing, light a candle, whatever.
As my Englishman penned, it's to be or not to be.
Don't drown your spirit in a bottle, helter-skelter.

I must counsel Lucille and Richie to aid Mo and Mick.
Miles to go before Mick arrives — his heart is jello.
Can I guide his mind, be his rock, be hip, be slick?
His family life was a sea sickness — a vertigo,

but... Praise Jahweh that's enough formality for today.
I must guide his alcoholic progress, be his sunray.

Mother's Day

(Heaven. Lucille listens to Richie but often disagrees.)

Yo, Ma! I got Peter's
dispen-sa-bull. Hey, he likes me.
Don't be pissed at me, Ma —
I just nodded out at the wheel —
hey, you cleared your own nose plenty.
Ma, give me a squeeze!

Ouch! That hurts my head.
I love you, Ma — cool to see you.
Ma, I tried like a fireman for Mo.
But she's got hooters like you —
I couldn't keep the homeboys off her.
I blew it. But there are cards to play!

Peter says Mick can free Mo
from the blackbirds
before she fries the convent.
Mick holds the wild cards! *(Lucille disbelieves.)*
Cards, I'm telling you,
not a Schnapps bottle... *(L shakes head.)*

Okay! Mick always has a bottle.
And a gorilla too — I heard it roaring.
I feel bad for Dad.
He never gets a night's rest. All he has
are nightmares, the gorilla, and me.
He tells weird stories...

Anyway, Ma, I love ya.
I can't visit Mo, but Peter says hope
is possible, if we believe.
He says we should forgive, and pray.
He says prayer worked for the Red Sox.
Prayer, and fastballs.

Who's on First

(Heaven. Richie paces about in frustration.)

I ain't sure what works, and Peter's
always watchin'. But I got some tricks
to catch some pigeons.

I'm schemin' to spring Mo
from the blackbirds. She's freakin'
like a Foo Dude.

I got to spy out
where that convent is. But I got
problems —

Ma is set against Mick but
if he rescues Mo, she may forgive him.
Who forgives me?

Peter says no problem — parents
screw up. He says kids always feel
guilty, says I ain't shot anyone, yet.

Mick's so full of shit — hippies,
'Nam, the Twisters... Then Billy G
shows up and I can't get a swear in!

I should'a stayed with Mo.
I was out scorin' cheeseburgers.

"Should'a, should'a, should'a" —
that's what Peter says. Like he's a freakin'
bishop or somethin'.

King of Central Park

(Central Park. Mick throws imaginary crumbs from a park bench and waves an American flag.)

I been hawkin' Stars and Stripes in Central Park
by the bandstand — Strawberry Fields, Central Park.

I been lurkin' like a lobster, like the King of Shame
in the bushes, on the bike path, in Central Park.

Losin' my kids, skippin' cops, I got no game.
Wavin' flags, wishin' I seen 'em, in Central Park.

I keep a neat pint in a brown bag just the same
'cause it keeps me nice and tight in Central Park.

Wet gray pigeons, hungry, always look the same,
feedin' off wrappers, bread crumbs in Central Park.

I wish I was a starter in the July All Star game,
but I'm a crate drunk in New York, in Central Park.

This sick smelly raggie tries not to forget his name —
Mick Monahan's the Viet vet works Central Park.

Blue Memories

(Heaven. Lucille waves American flag.)

If I didn't have my brats
I'd have modeled for *Vogue*.
I had the bust for it,
the bones, the skinny face. But Mick
knocked me up. The Army
drafted him. I waited.
While he was in 'Nam
I paid the abortion.

We used to party at the Fillmore.
Mick camped there weekends.
He'd sneak me in a side door —
we'd smoke enormous yellow
hash bongs in the balcony.
Imagine — Mick an usher.
He couldn't find his flashlight
but he found me, all right.

Those psychedelic lightshows —
the Youngbloods, Airplane,
Grateful Dead. I could sing
like Grace Slick, I swear. Mick
worked Woodstock — I wish
I was there. Mick hanging
off his scaffold and waving
his flag. *(L waves, then drops her flag.)*

If I had quit my habit and the Trade
Center job, I could have raised
Mo and Rich — they were my rubies,
my gorgeous birthstones.
If, if, only if...I kick myself...
Peter warns me — don't be bitter.

Ortiz the Detective

(109th Street. Mick sleeps. Ortiz studies baseball cards from his wallet.)

What bubblegum beauties
he carries around with him —
Micky Mantle's Triple Crown, Yogi MVP,
Gil Hodges, Duke Snyder, Mays
with his backward basket catch.

This bum must have been someone,
a player. His crate's inked, indelible black —
"Home of Champions." A ball player
or he's made himself a Wheaties hero —
drunks hallucinate. Loud loose shotguns.

Fact — I'm up for a hearing. Sarge
and Bloomberg broom the streets clean.
No gold shield now for me.
No promotion, no pension.

But look at these moldy classics —
Johnny Podres throwing the 7th game
of the '55 Series. The one year
the Brooklyn Dodgers beat the Yankees.
Jackie stealing home on Berra,
Yogi jumping up and down screaming!

I suspect he has more rare cards.
There's a hot market for these collectibles.
I'll run them past a pawnbroker I know.
Here's two wrinkled baby pictures too.
This rumpot is someone's father!
His baby boy has his pointy ears.

I Wish I Was Mariano Rivera

(Heaven. A blown-up photo of a Red Hummer hangs overhead.)

If I was Mariano Rivera
nobody would *ever* fuck with me.
I'd buzz a fastball
right past St. P's good ear
and sink one just below his belt —
"Strike three!"

Flashbulbs would be poppin'
as I fly around the galaxy
in a Hummer. A special order
red Hummer to go with my hair.
I'd call it "Bummer Hummer"
so nobody'd get in my way.

I'd pitch my father
into the Hall of Heaven.
Saint Peter says trust in God,
not greenbacks. Like he's a guru
or somethin'. Faith, he says, keep faith.
I got faith in Rivera. He's my hero.

Lucille Hits Her Knees

(Heaven. Lucille delivers her soliloquy to the audience.)

There's nothing to be done for Richie —
my baby lost his head. It bounced up here.
But why can't Mo go to a good school
where she could study things
the nuns don't think are good for her?
My second baby deserves a second chance.

I don't trust the black habit nuns —
I was abused as a hippie girl
in Sacred Heart. The rote, the uniforms,
whacks across my palm with the ruler.
They exorcised my sins, they thought,
but Mick and I were joined bad asses.

I almost wish the Sisters had won
so we two couldn't live our wild party.
We were split apart too late to be saved.
I wish my life had been long enough for me
to shelter my baby daughter.
Now her only prayer is Mick. He's hopeless.

Richie squawks in Mick's ear —
Peter says it's "proactive." But poor Mick's
just a beat-up bankrupt bum.
He's quicksand — no rainbow there.
Who is there for me to trust? Peter says
to forgive is divine. That grace isn't mine —

except I'd forgive Monahan all his flaws
if Mo could go to a school without guns and
horny homeboys jumping her bones.
My fault — I was too hot for my own health
and hers too, I fear. Don't be too good looking.
It's bad karma, and not just for you.

Dear God, please hear my prayer —
Let someone see Mo's genius. What angel
with shiny star will rescue my daughter?
Please let there be a joyful ending!
What does Richie's prattle mean? Wild cards?
A joker in Heaven? Please, angel, appear!

CURTAIN AND INTERMISSION

Act 4

Seventh Inning Stretch

CRAZY LIKE A FOX

(109th Street. Mick talks to Ortiz, who walks back and forth.)

Buenos noches, 1-8-3-1 Ortiz.
Hola, officer, and to what

do I owe the honor of you again? *(Ortiz offers imaginary wallet)*
Jesus! You found my wallet? *(Ortiz pantomimes speech.)*

My box? The wallet was in it all along?
So show it to Sergeant Big Shit...

All right, all right, I'm not bitchin' —
I've got my photos back, and my old cards. *(Ortiz mimes)*

Yes, that's Richie — and that's my girl,
Maureen. I called her little Mo before...

My cards keep me happy now, that's all. *(Ortiz mimes)*
Do I have more? Who wants to know?

I hallucinate, you know.
These bubblegum pictures are worthless,

all ripped and smudged to shit. *(Ortiz pantomimes speech.)*
You think I stashed some good ones, huh?

That's it? Money? What's your cut?
I got nothin' — baseball cards and baby shoes.

Adios. Let me sleep.
I'm not Fort Knox. God bless, boy-o.
(Mick clilmbs back into his cardboard.)

Trophies

(The Bleachers. Mick studies baseball cards.)

I keep 'em safe in my shoebox,
I look at 'em when I'm alone.

Jackie Robinson — I traded
Joe D. for him.

Duke Snyder, Gil Hodges,
Pee Wee Reese and Campy,

Sandy Koufax, Bob Feller,
Teddy Ballgame at Fenway...

I got 'em all when I was small,
flipped 'em and traded 'em —

Hammerin' Hank Aaron, Drysdale
and "Lefty" — Steve Carlton.

That's who I was,
who I wanted to be

when the sun burned my neck
and sweat ran off me like a hydrant

and I was beating it out to first,
stealing second, takin' the big lead,

roundin' third, streakin' home
and safe! Safe! Just like Jackie!

I was the MVP, I was Yogi,
I was Clemente — all those guys...

(Mick returns the cards to his shoebox and carefully places the shoebox in his pack.)

But I lost it. Now all I got is ripped
cards, and maybe — Ortiz.

Ortiz on Watch

(109th Street. Ortiz watches while Mick sleeps in his cardboard. A large metal cross hangs over him.)

I keep an eye on his Maytag crate
while he snores. His son Richie
decapitated, mother burned. Is his foul
rant real? What's his hallucination?
Fact: his lungs are shot, he's wheezing.
Fact: he lost his right hand at Lai Khe.

I should have been crushed myself.
September morning sun, bright blue sky,
trolling for stripers off Brooklyn.
Then smoke spewing black ash
over Manhattan. When I got there, what
to do? I wrapped the dogs' bloody paws.

Fact: my day off. My shift and precinct got it.
I shoveled rubble and razor sharp metal
with ironworkers, hardhats on chests.
We found body parts under concrete.
I'm guessing Mick's wife was there.
Did my partner die trying to save her?

Most just disappeared, atomized.
Fifty-two cops, thirteen EMTs,
three hundred forty-three firemen.
When I think of them, I think of Mick.
I see the cross of twisted
steel beams dangling right over him.

Kill the Messenger

(109th Street. Mick crawls out from his cardboard, rubs head, sounds manic.)

Jesus, what a potato head I got — Smirnoff
straight is mashed potato brains. *(Richie's head appears.)*

And if a Major League hangover ain't
enough, here's little redhead to harangue me.

Who asked you down today? Hey?
You want a slug of my fist? I'm finished

telling you my story. Up to here with you!
Take your Peter baloney and stick it up

your Hummer. I'm gonna buy a loaf
of day-old Wonder Bread, picnic with my pigeons

in Central Park. I'm givin' a concert
at the Band Shell. Singin' "Blue Monday"

to my birdy buds. I'll sell hundreds of red
white and blues by the crook of my hook!

If my cards are worth two bucks
or five hundred or whatever, they're sold.

I'll deal the mess to the first cash collector,
then we'll sing our hearts out, my buds and me.

I'll feed 'em fresh croissants and myself
a magnum of Corboiser! A cognac drunk!

Haven't sucked that since I lived with Lucille.
I'll drown with my stinkin' gorilla in ninety-

proof! Gimme some bucks and a bottle.
Let's light this rocket! Just watch me.

Richie Pulls the Fire Alarm

Heaven. Peter raises his staff to indicate his displeasure with Richie's lack of faith and occasionally smacks him.)

Hey Peter, smoke's risin'!
Mick's reelin' for a drunk,
Mo's locked up
and I'm freakin'!

Billy Gorilla's loose,
Lucille's PMS'ing,
no sign of Ortiz,
no loaves, no fishes, *nada*!

I hope you got a white rabbit
in that fat wood stick
or at least gold angels
with hundred dollar bills

'cause there's bubbly black
tar on the roof.
I don't see no hope
for Mick or Mo, Lucille or me.

Mick's gonna play
his wild cards, he says.
He's gonna deal 'em
all for booze. Jesus!

OW! OW!
He'll piss the bucks
on bourbon! He's plotting
the toot of all time!

Whatd'ya mean
"little head, little faith"?
Show me the miracle!
Make 109th Street

bright like Broadway!
Raise the ladders!
Turn on the hydrants!
Sirens! Send the fire trucks!

Saint Peter's Crystal Ball

(Heaven. Peter stares into a crystal ball. Richie appears. Peter addresses him.)

I proclaim the rule of Yahweh and Mohammed,
Buddha, Christ, Rabbi Rubin, and yes, U-2.
I raise my staff to stop the ravaging and rumors spread
to break God's laws. That means you too,
little Red Head. You think this is the Lower East Side?
You've been watching a Hollywood cowboy movie!
The Spirit is driving — we're all just along for the ride.
Everyone's singin' the blues. I hear 'em loud and groovy!

Let me cut to the chase, reform this crazy place,
predict how it ends — in the place of innocent grace.
Maureen's future is the x in our eloquent equation.
I foresee she will have an Inexplicable Misconception,
and Mick will see a light, or perhaps a pawn shop.
Ortiz is my Blue Angel, city man of law, hero cop.

Mick Sees the Light

(109th Street. Ortiz shines flashlight on Mick.)

Jesus! It's the end. I'm croaked!
Stop sticking that damn light in my eyes!

You again, blue devil. *(Listens)* You have *not*!
(Listens) You have? Where is she?

Jesus, tell me and I'll go to her.
Right now! Wait, she can't see me like this.

Jesus, I'm fucked. I stink like a mutt.
I don't want Mo to see her daddy so ragged.

(Listens) My cards could be worth *how much?*
Well, fuck me. I mean how do you know?

(Listens) You can pawn them? We can spring Mo?
What's your share? *(Listens)* Now you're talkin'.

We'll bust her out like a jailbreak... *(Listens)* No?
A better plan? You're asking too much... *(Listens)*

All right, take 'em. *(Hands over cards)* Now kill that light
and fuck off. I ain't been clean for years.

Immaculate Misconception

*(The Convent. Nuns in background.
Maureen holds Bible and iPod.)*

I rocked to sleep with a belly ache.
Good Friday my eyes popped open —
my belly shrunk, empty inside!
No one knows where Baby went.

The nuns say I'm a Magdalene
but I only dreamed two Barbie Dolls
and my big brother. Where is Richie?
I have nightmares he crashed a truck.

The Carmelites searched my dresser,
called in the Jesuits. Mother Superior
stole my stuff, strip-searched me —
no hangers, no blood, no fetus.

Why did I dream about my dollies?
I dreamed a brown man held them,
a policeman. He smelled like soap.
He saved babies Jessica and Jolie.

I never told the nuns, I just read on —
I memorize one holy psalm each day.
The Old Testament is what I like.
I know "Ecclesiastes" by heart.

*I know that whatever God does
it will be forever: nothing can be put
to it, nor anything taken from it; and
God does it, that men fear before Him.*

Million Dollar Drunk

(ER. Doctor & nurse alternate.)

Pneumonia,
blood alcohol 1.7.
He's aspirating,
vomit in one lung.

A lung abscess,
hypothermia.
He passed out
in the snow.

He fills Intensive Care
with complications —
maybe hit by a bus,
this stumblebum.

Fractured skull —
subdural hematoma
will kill him.
Delirium Tremens too.

Liver lacks
white blood cells.
Labs show
cirrhosis, Hep-C.

Liver cancer?
Where will he go?
He'll be back,
bankrupt the ER.

CURTAIN

Act 5

Last Licks

Good Samaritan

*(109th Street. Ortiz wakes Mick from stupor,
leans close to him.)*

What a stink! A dead fish,
white like a turnip.
Listen, Mick.
There's blood in your ear.

I sold the box for a hundred large
and prepaid Mo's expenses,
found her a place at Hotchkiss School,
knew a Big Shot who owed me a favor.

See my hand? Take
the pen, sign this Power
of Attorney — I'll represent you.
Look, we'll free Maureen!

We're going back to the ER now.
Trust me on this, please.
Let's try Saint Luke's — it's close.
You've met the Chief of Trauma?

Mo Dreams of Mick

(Hotchkiss School. Greek columns. Mo peers behind Mick's cardboard where he's hiding, hunched behind Ortiz. Mick turns his face away from Mo.)

The man is hard to see — smudged,
hiding behind a cardboard shack.
He whistles, he wants to talk to me.
But I can't hear what he whispers.

He's with Dove, the policeman
who saved my dollies. Dove is huge
and brown in that new charcoal suit.
He says I'm going to Hotchkiss School!

Is that my father? Why does he
hide his face from me? Don't
be afraid — I won't curse you.
You're shy — and you need a shave.

I think you are my father —
I want to see you, please.
Why do you turn your face away?
Don't you love me, Daddy?

Mea Culpa

(ER Room. Doctor stands silently on one side, nurse on the other. Mick speaks to Ortiz, who hovers by him.)

1. Deny It

You promised to move me but can't.
I want to visit Mo. I'm okay! Liar!
White coat liars! Cops and snotty silk-
tie doctors with x-rays and asshole
remarks — "Here's Pops Moonshine
again. A pint of Muscat in a pack."
Fuck you! Fuck them! You're wrong!
You itty-titty nurses with slick hair,
big asses. Special 'cause you got
blue scrubs, panty lines and diamonds.
I keyed all the gleamy SUVs parked
by the "Reserved for Doctors" sign.
I'll reserve a place for you, I will!
Right where your flashlights don't shine.

2. Fuckin' A Angry

I should bomb your sneering Sergeant
and his whole pussy-blue jailhouse
and bastard Lieutenant Brown in 'Nam
and naggin' Lucille, and especially you,
Ortiz! I don't deserve none of this!
I worked my ass off! I graduated
Sacred Heart, survived Lai Khe too.
I played for the Torrington Twisters.
I never got a chance to prove myself.
If I told you all the women I knew
there'd be a chorus line down Broadway
and lots of pissed-off husbands,
curious sisters, too. It's not my time!
I won't die here! Jesus H. Christ!

3. Let's Make a Deal

Can we work somethin' out here?
It ain't over till it's over. Remember
Yogi and the bottom ninth line-drive
home runs he hit? I was sittin' rootin'
in the right field bleachers — CRACK!
he whacks it smack off the foul pole!
I swear I got a comeback in me too. I got
bundles of cash — you moved the cards.
I got a bona fida motivation to sober up.
My sweet Maureen... I'll visit her
at Hotchkiss, sign her report cards.
I just want time to see Mo's graduation.
Don't leave me here at St. Luke's.
You ER doctors, save me. Please.

4. Depression

If I won't live, then I don't care.
My kids? I think I dreamed them up.
I don't think none of this is real —
especially you in a black pimp suit,
listening like a priest. This is Deliriums.
Ortiz, are you real? Hear me? Care?
Yes? God forgive. Did I ever say I'm sorry?
Ah, fuck it. There's nothing to be fixed
for what I did. I got smashed and I did it
and I'm sorry. I admit it. Lucille
heaved her iron skillet at my head and
it's black Irish luck she missed.
Jesus, what a mess I made of my life!
I try to sleep all day but you won't let me.

5. Acceptance

I'll sign the guardian paper.
Ortiz, you're an *amigo*.
Thanks for freeing Mo.
Thank God her money's in trust.
Wish I met her. Please tell her —
explain I was sick. That's the truth.
Make Mo listen to her teachers,
be the major leaguer I couldn't be.
I had lots of at-bats, just didn't hit shit,
never hit the rocket when it counted.
I kept tryin' to pull it, hit the big ones.
Never got around — too scared, too slow.
Finally I just ran out of strikes.
Don't let Mo make my mistakes.

Last At Bat

(The ER. Mick has Ortiz pull Yankee shirt from his pack.)

If you would dig in my pack for me —
I want to give you my souvenir shirt.
I knew Billy Martin with The Twisters.
He mailed this to me after he went up.
He was a scrapper, our second baseman,
a wonderful drinker, World Series winner.
Now I'm passing Yankee luck to you.
The pinstripes go with your black suit.
I got no final thoughts, no sugar wishes.
I believe I used the tough breaks I had.
I just wish I had more time for Mo.
I never quit on her, just left it here. Mister
Branch Rickey said, "Don't whine, run
out everything. Leave it all on the field."

Prayer from The Bleachers

(The Bleachers. Richie speaks, wearing a backward Yankees cap and holding his yellow mitt.)

These wooden bleachers smell like Hell —
crushed peanut shells and crackerjacks,
beer cups and hot dogs. *Boom! Boom!*
Us bleacher bums stomp our feet, the concrete
rocks — the Sox figure it's "Ballgame."
Please God, don't let my Dad strike out!

Look God, your Brooklyn boy is shiverin',
rootin' for a rally, cap on backwards.
Mick's scorecard is full of strike-outs. But
pitch Mick a cookie, let him hit it hard and far
to right, a line drive to me. Yogi Berra said
it ain't over till it's over. And he's important.

It's too black to see the scoreboard. Don't
dim the lights on Yankee Stadium's roof.
Let me play catch with Mick again. Pull it
here, Dad. I'm squeezin' the old Wilson
catcher's mitt you gave me. Crush the ball —
I want to snare it in this yellow glove.

CURTAIN

ACT 6

EXTRA INNINGS

Gate Keeper

(Heaven. Red neon lights flash on and off. Mick faces St. Peter.)

Mick Monahan! I welcome you to Heaven and accept your plea.
Guilty. I don't hear that often. 109th and Amsterdam was hell?
Well, judging by your pallor, I'd say you slipped and fell.
But Lucifer's flames are bluer than you. Of course that's just me
speaking, Peter Lie Detector, if you haven't the eyes to see
my sign. Red neon reads *Pause ye who would enter here and tell
your truth, the whole truth and nothing but the truth.* My alarm bell
rings if you speak false. Now, I pray, be brief. Please bend a knee.

(Mick kneels and pantomimes speech.)

I see. I see. And would you say, if you had your life to do over,
you would change anything? *(pause)* Yes, I see. Yes I do understand.
Do you know your son submitted a mercy plea for you to join us?
I've allowed Richie and Lucille to visit you, you sad Irish Rover.
And while I deliberate, spin them your story, not boastful or grand.
Richie will taxi you all in the Hummer to see Mo at Hotchkiss.

Alternative Energy Vehicle

*(Heaven. Mick, Lucille and Richie all sit
in a red Hummer. The angel who announces
each title pops up behind the Hummer)*

Yo, Ma! Fasten your seat belt!
I'm steerin' us to Connecticut!
Here's Mick, Ma. He won't show
his face. He got cold toes.

I got the juice, if you got a map.
Pedal to the metal, erase this place!
(Listens.)
Whatd'ya mean, we gotta be back?
Oh, yeah. I almost forgot.

We'll all see Mo at Hotchkiss.
She got a skirt and penny loafers.
They got four soccer fields!
They got porches, Greek columns.

You sit in back with Mick, Ma.
I'll fly us to Lakeville in no time.
Red Hummer runs on hydrogen.
Good old Peter loaned me the key.

Terms of Endearment

*(Heaven. Lucille addresses Mick from
back seat of the Hummer.)*

Well, Mick, long years no see.
You're not looking swell but
I was dead when I got here too.
What's wrong? Rat got your tongue?
You weren't shy before. In fact
I couldn't keep you off me. What's
the verdict? I did promise Peter
I'd forgive you. But forgetting
is another book. I'll work at it.
That's my Lenten Resolution.

While you were in Reception
copping your plea, I looked
down on Mo. She got "A"s
in Latin and Spanish. And your cop
got canned. They took his badge
and he's off on a binge of his own.
You see your effect on people.
Good thinking he invested the money
for Maureen, first. Or I'd go back,
beat a penance from him. You too.

Re your final address, leave me out.
I don't want the boy learning details
of our East Side civil war. He is a boy,
fifteen in human years, but he thinks
he talked Peter into this Red Hummer.
There's no vehicular traffic up here,
an occasional lost satellite but we scoot
right past it. Whatever else you tell him,
don't tell Richie this tank is an angel
in disguise. Peter's very good that way.

Just look at our rascal up front —
he has moose ears like you — they point
straight up when he's listening.
Pay attention to your driving, Richie!
I'll make him behave or my name's
not Lucille. Lucille Sheedy Monahan.
You know I never had money for a divorce
so you better behave or I won't bake
your favorite cinnamon rolls.
Or give you any other treats!

Letter to Mr. Ortiz

*(Hotchkiss. Mo speaks to Ortiz,
who stands stage left.)*

Dear Mr. Ortiz,
are you sure my mom
died with your partner?
No one ever found them.

I dream some nights
about my mom. I'm sure
I see my father too.
He hides his face from me.

And my brother Richie... *(Listens)*
Are you sure? Twice
I told him *Don't steal.*
I miss my family.

Mr. Ortiz —
I love it here.
You don't answer my letters.
I hope you're happy too.

Do you study clouds?
(The Red Hummer appears stage right.)
I wish you saw this sunset!
And right over the dorm
is a cool red jeep.

Ballgame

(Heaven. St. Peter speaks.)

It's lights out when Aretha starts to sing.
After hearing her I got a text memo from The Boss —
Mick the homeless yahoo did lose everything
but he was a ballpark hotdog, not a loss —
a frankfurter low on nutrition but full of relish,
with a mustard, catsup, sauerkraut garnish.
He sold his shoebox to save his daughter.
Hey, I've admitted drunks who don't hold water.
Let him in, yes, let him in, let him ride!
Make a place in the Hall for this good old sinner!
He didn't plan his head-first bellyflop slide.
He played his trump cards, came out a winner.
You're in with Flynn, Mister Mick Monahan!
Pick a uniform number. I, Peter, lift your ban!

(Peter does a jig.)

Lucky Number One!

(Heaven. Mick, Lucille and Richie roll on stage in the Red Hummer. Mick speaks.)

I don't know what Lucille and Richie like me to say.
I'd probably say it wrong anyway. Don't know

how to explain wanting them to find me, help me.
I never expected to get here. Is this my last fuck-up?

After Lai Khe I couldn't swing a framing hammer,
never mind a bat. No work, no play for an amputee.

Flashbacks kept coming. The V.A. didn't help.
I fell into a fifth of Dewars and drowned. Just like that.

But Richie found me — he never gave up.
And Ortiz figured I had the right cards.

I hope Mo can help Ortiz — he's an Iraq vet.
We serve, we're shot, we're fucked, so what?

Who knows how the hardball bounces, or where?
Who knows the final score? All our service —

why? But I lucked out, worked a walk, ball four,
came all the way around to score. My number

isn't up. It's *on* me! Lucille, we got Series tickets!
Richie, rock this fire truck to Heaven! Play ball!

CURTAIN

About the Author

Jim Kelleher teaches literature and composition at Northwestern Community College in Winsted, Connecticut, works in a group home to support three handicapped men, and is also a self-employed carpentry contractor. He earned an MFA degree from New England College in 2007. In former lives he was a teacher in the Boston public schools, caretaker for a summer camp, and Fillmore East usher. His first poetry collection, *Quarry*, was published by Antrim House in 2008. Jim Kelleher lives with Queenie Troy in Goshen, Connecticut.

This book is set in Arial, a contemporary sans serif typeface designed in 1982 by a ten-person team led by Robin Nicholas and Patricia Saunders. The overall treatment of curves in Arial is softer and fuller than in most sans serif faces. Terminal strokes are cut on the diagonal, which helps to "humanize" the font.

To order additional copies of this book
or other Antrim House titles, contact the publisher at

Antrim House
21 Goodrich Rd., Simsbury, CT 06070
860.217.0023, AntrimHouse@comcast.net
or the house website (www.AntrimHouseBooks.com).

•

On the house website
are sample poems, upcoming events, links,
and a "seminar room" featuring supplemental biography,
notes, images, poems, reviews, and
writing suggestions.